10-23-98

To: Tyler

From: Grandma

Practice Makes Perfect!

Henry's Baby

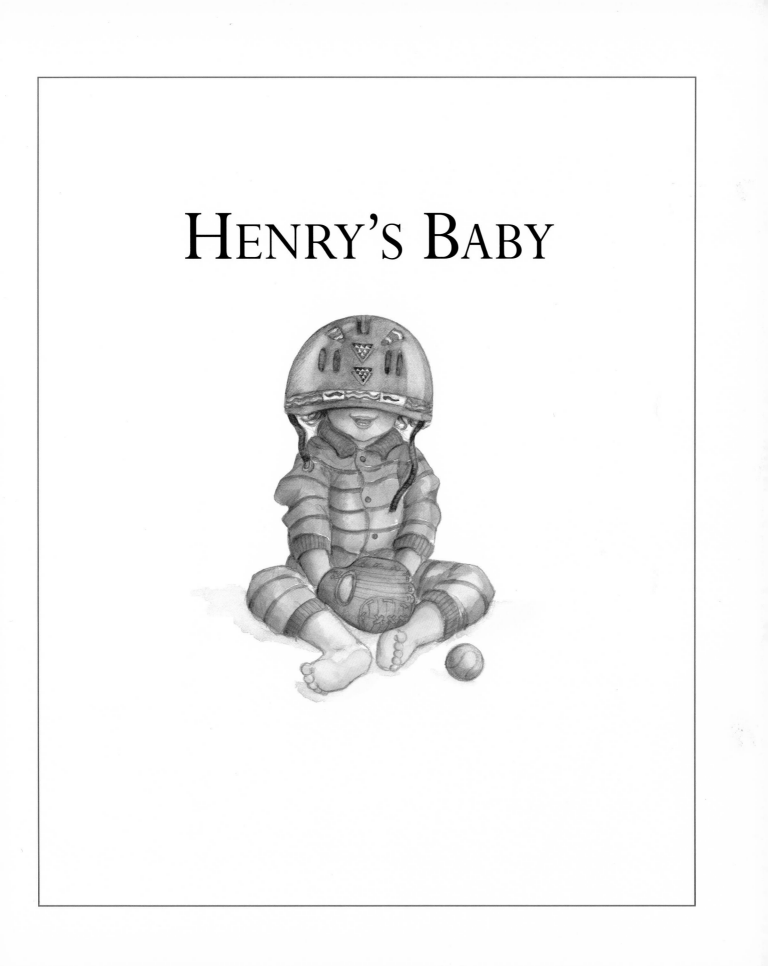

For Julia Eccleshare,
whose Henry and George inspired the story.

DK

A DORLING KINDERSLEY BOOK

First American Edition, 1993
2 4 6 8 10 9 7 5 3 1

Published in the United States by
Dorling Kindersley, Inc., 232 Madison Avenue
New York, New York 10016

Library of Congress Cataloging-in-Publication Data
Hoffman, Mary, 1945-
     Henry's baby / by Mary Hoffman: illustrated by Susan Winter. –
1st American ed.
          p. cm.
     Summary: When Henry has the "in" crowd from school over to
his house, he worries that his baby brother will ruin the afternoon.
     ISBN 1-56458-196-9
     [1. Popularity – Fiction. 2. Babies – Fiction. 3. Brothers –
Fiction.] I. Winter, Susan, ill. II. Title.
PZ7.H67562He   1993
[E] –dc20   92-53485
                                                                        CIP
                                                                         AC

Color reproduction by DOT Gradations Ltd.
Printed in Belgium by Proost

HENRY'S
BABY

Mary
Hoffman

Illustrated by
Susan Winter

DORLING KINDERSLEY
LONDON • NEW YORK • STUTTGART

There was only one gang that Henry Moon wanted to belong to at his new school. They didn't have a name or a password. The teachers called them "that bunch." The kids just said "Them."

Henry wanted to be one of Them so badly, it hurt.
The trouble was, there was nothing special about Henry.

Every member of the gang had something special about him. Skif was the trendy one. He had all the latest clothes, knew all the latest songs, and had a boom box so big it made him walk crooked.

Henry had a decent pair of sneakers and a tracksuit in the right color, but he only had a secondhand personal stereo that he wasn't allowed to bring to school.

The Prof was a computer-head. His Dad let him play games late into the night and he always had state-of-the-art software, often before it arrived in the stores. Henry had an educational computer program.
His parents were not big on the Prof's kind of games.

Daniel was the best at running,
jumping, swimming, and baseball.
His friends called him Zip. Henry
was on the local swim team and had
a baseball glove signed by Nolan
Ryan, but he wasn't in Zip's league.

Jake was the tough man. He had more muscles than some of the teachers and could stop a fight just by rolling up his sleeves. (Sometimes he started fights that way, too.)

Henry was not a weakling, but he didn't have muscles like Jake's.

What Henry had was a baby.

Henry didn't mind the baby; in fact he sort of liked him. And the baby thought Henry was the greatest kid in the world.

Whenever Henry felt down, he would put baby George on his lap and play "This is the way the baby rides." It was George's favorite game, making him giggle 'til he hiccuped. "Again!" was the first word George ever said, because he always wanted to be bounced some more on Henry's lap.

Yes, as babies go, George was okay.

It was just that a baby didn't
really fit Henry's image.
Or the image he wished he had.

Tough. Cool. *Interesting.*

Then one day at school, the Prof unexpectedly asked Henry if he'd like to see his latest computer game. Henry was rapt. He started going over to the Prof's house once a week. But Henry never asked him over to *his* house. Henry didn't want the Prof to know he had a baby.

Then Henry took second to Zip in the freestyle swim race at the pool. And Zip asked if he'd like to go to the Water Park with him on Sunday morning. Together they went to the new park, which had a water slide and a wave machine!

The next day, Jake said hi to
Henry during recess and Skif waved a lazy
hand. It was great. Henry felt almost like one of Them.

There was no system of joining. You were either one of Them,
or you weren't. Henry knew that They met every Wednesday
after school in one another's houses. But he didn't know what
else They did.

Then one Tuesday at school, Skif came up to Henry, clicking his fingers to a rhythm he was hearing in his head.

"Hey, Moonshine!" he called out, holding his hand out for five. Henry was so surprised, he almost forgot to slap Skif's hand.

"We've got a problem," said Skif.

He explained that They couldn't meet at his house the next day because his mom had some friends coming over to try on bridesmaids' dresses. The Prof's dad had a work meeting at their house, it was Zip's sister's birthday party, and Jake's living room was being repainted.

"So," said Skif, with a big grin, "we wondered about going to your place."

This was it! Henry's big chance. They wanted to meet at his house! If he made the right impression, he would be *in*.

"Mom," he asked that night, "is it all right if I bring some friends over after school tomorrow?"

"Fine," said Mom, who was spooning oatmealy goo into the baby. "I'm glad you're making friends."

"The thing is," said Henry, "they might be a bit noisy for George."

"I see," said Mom. "Don't worry. I'm taking George next door tomorrow—we're going to visit with Ann and baby Tom. You and your friends will have the place to yourselves." And she gave Henry a wink.

"Yes!" thought Henry. "I'm *in!*"

But on Wednesday, disaster struck. The gang hadn't been at Henry's house for more than ten minutes when his mom rushed in . . .
holding the baby.

"I'm sorry, Henry," she gasped, "but you'll have to watch George for me. Tom swallowed an earring and I need to drive him and Ann to the hospital. It won't be for long. Dad's on his way home." She dumped George in Henry's arms and rushed out before he had time to say a word.

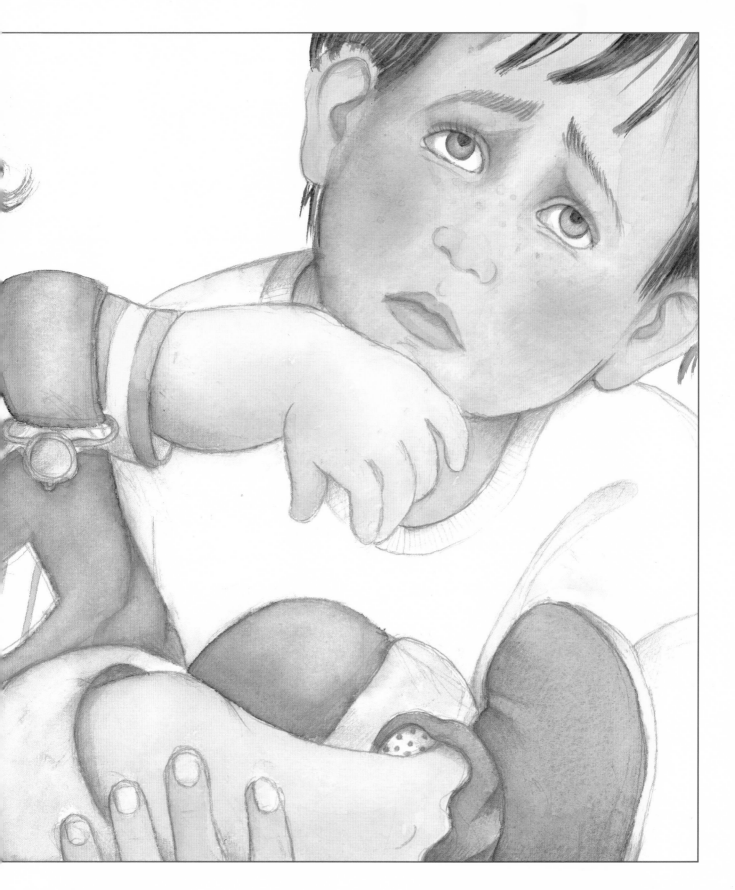

There was a stunned silence while
the gang looked at George.
"Hey," said Jake, "you never said
you had a baby."

Henry wondered wildly whether to lie and say
that his mom was baby-sitting George for
someone else. But everyone always said that
the baby looked just like Henry.

Jake came closer and took a good look at George.
George was a friendly baby. He reached his fat hands out
wide and gave Jake one of his best sloppy kisses.

Henry hastily put George in his high chair and mixed up some of his baby cereal, trying not to look at Jake.

"Can I try that?" asked Skif, and soon he was spooning oatmeal into George, regardless of the amount that was getting on his brand-new sweatshirt. The trendiest kid in school was beginning to look like the swamp monster.

Next, Henry put George in his playpen and he started one of his favorite games of throwing out all his toys. But champion catcher Zip fielded every one. "Owzat!" he shouted every time, and George giggled.

26

"That is one smart baby," said the Prof, polishing his glasses. "We could study him, you know – use a graphics program and chart his growth and development. It would make a good project.

By the time Henry's mom got home, the boys were all leaving. "I'm sorry, Henry," she whispered, "for spoiling your afternoon."

"Thanks for the cookies, Mrs. Moon," said the Prof. "We had a great time."

"Yeah," said Jake. "Can we have our meeting here next Wednesday, too?"

And they did.

Henry is one of Them now. He still isn't anything special. He isn't the cleverest kid or the toughest or the trendiest and he isn't the best athlete. . . .

But he *is* the only one with a baby.